POKÉMON™

PIKACHU'S VACATION

There are more books
about Pokémon.

Collect them all!

#1 I Choose You!
#2 Island of the Giant Pokémon
#3 Attack of the Prehistoric Pokémon
#4 Night in the Haunted Tower

coming soon

#5 Team Rocket Blasts Off!

Movie novelizations

Mewtwo Strikes Back

Pikachu's Vacation

POKÉMON

PIKACHU'S VACATION

MOVIE ADAPTATION BY
TRACEY WEST

SCHOLASTIC INC.

New York   Toronto   London   Auckland   Sydney
Mexico City   New Delhi   Hong Kong

No part of this work may be reproduced, stored in a retrieval system, or transmitted in any form or by any means, electronic, mechanical, photocopying, recording, or otherwise, without written permission of the publisher. For information regarding permission, write to Scholastic Inc., Attention: Permissions Department, 555 Broadway, New York, NY 10012.

ISBN 0-439-15986-5

12 11 10 9 8 7   9/9 0 1 2 3 4/0

Printed in the U.S.A.
First Scholastic printing, November 1999

Table of Contents

Poké Talk

Check out these words before you read the book.

Pokémon: These creatures have special powers. There are more than 151 kinds of Pokémon in the world.

Pokémon trainer: A boy or girl who catches and takes care of Pokémon. Trainers use their Pokémon in battles against other Pokémon.

Poké Ball: A small red-and-white ball. Most Pokémon live in these balls until their trainers call them out. Trainers can use their Poké Balls to catch new Pokémon.

Electric Pokémon: They have electric shock powers. Electric Pokémon use lightning to defeat other Pokémon.

Water Pokémon: Most of them live in water. They have skills like Bubble and Water Gun.

Poison Pokémon: These Pokémon use poison in their attacks to make other Pokémon sick.

Flying Pokémon: Most Flying Pokémon have wings. Some look like birds or dragons.

Rock Pokémon: They are made of rocks and come in all shapes and sizes.

Evolution: Pokémon do not stay the same forever. They learn and grow. When they have learned enough new skills, they change. They evolve. For example, Pikachu evolves into Raichu.

CHAPTER ONE

Pokémon Playground

"We are here," Ash Ketchum said. "We are at the Pokémon Playground!"

"*Pika!*" Pikachu smiled at Ash, its trainer. The little yellow Pokémon gazed up at the playground. It looked like a big brown mountain.

"All Pokémon can have fun and play here," said Ash's friend Misty.

"Yes," said Ash's friend Brock. "All Pokémon need to take a break once in a while."

Pikachu smiled at the three Pokémon trainers. Pikachu liked traveling around with them. But today was a special day. Today was a day to have fun with friends. It was Pikachu's vacation.

"Pikachu! Pikachu!" Pikachu said. Its red cheeks glowed with excitement.

Ash understood. He took a Poké Ball from his belt.

"Pikachu wants us to let our other Pokémon out of their Poké Balls," Ash said.

One by one, Ash took out his Poké Balls. He pressed a button on each ball. Bright lights flashed.

Flash! First came Bulbasaur, the Pokémon with the plant bulb on its back.

Flash! Then came Squirtle, which looked like a cute turtle.

Flash! Pidgeotto came out and flapped its wings.

Flash! Charizard flew out and shot fire from its mouth.

Misty took out her Poké Balls next. She called on her Water Pokémon, Goldeen and Staryu. Goldeen looked like a pretty orange fish. Staryu looked like a starfish with a jewel in its middle.

Then Misty called on Psyduck, the Pokémon that looked like a duck.

Then it was Brock's turn. He took out his Rock Pokémon, Onix and Geodude. Then Zubat flew out of its Poké Ball. Zubat looked like a blue bat. Last came Vulpix, the Pokémon that looked like a brown fox.

Pikachu was happy. All its friends were here. But someone was missing.

"Pikachu!" Pikachu told Misty.

Misty reached into her backpack.

"How could I forget?" she said. She took a tiny Pokémon called Togepi out of her backpack. This Pokémon had hatched from an egg that Ash found. It still had the eggshell on the bottom of its round body. Tiny arms and legs stuck out from the shell.

"*Togi! Togi!*" chirped Togepi in a high voice.

"We will meet you back here," Ash told Pikachu. "I am counting on you to look after the others."

"Especially Togepi," Misty said.

"*Pika! Pi.*" Pikachu would make Ash proud. It would take good care of its friends.

This was going to be the best day ever!

CHAPTER TWO

Pikachu's First Problem

A long walkway led to the
Pokémon Playground. Pikachu
walked down the trail. Goldeen
and Staryu swam in a stream next
to the trail. The other Pokémon
walked or flew behind Pikachu.

Ash, Misty, and Brock waved to

the Pokémon. "Good-bye! Have fun!" they called out.

Soon Pikachu and the others came to the entrance of the Pokémon Playground. Curved paths led up the big mountain. Fields of green grass covered the bottom of the mountain. Pikachu could see a swimming pool up ahead. Other Pokémon were playing in the pool.

"*Onix!*" Onix pushed its big stone body up the trail. Brock's Pokémon followed.

Goldeen and Staryu splashed into the pool.

Pidgeotto flew to the top of a tall tree. Charizard flew even higher, to the top of the mountain.

"Psy aye aye." Psyduck waddled around. It looked like it did not know where it wanted to go.

Pikachu turned to Squirtle and Bulbasaur.

"Pika? Pika?" Pikachu asked its friends what they should do first.

Sniff. Sniff.

What was making that sound?

Pikachu turned around. It was Togepi. The little Pokémon made a sad face.

"Waaaaaaaaah!" Togepi wailed. Tears poured from its cheeks. *"Waaaaaaah!"*

"Pika!" Pikachu was worried. Togepi was just a baby. It was hungry. Pikachu had to get Togepi to stop crying. But how?

Pikachu had an idea. It made a funny face. It pulled on its red cheeks. It wiggled its pointy ears.

Togepi's cries got softer.

The funny faces were working!

"Squirtle, squirt!"

Squirtle wanted to help, too. Squirtle pushed Pikachu out of the way.

"Squirtle!" Squirtle stuck out its tongue.

"Waaaaaah!" Togepi wailed even louder.

Squirtle looked sad. It did not want to make Togepi cry!

Pikachu thought and thought. They had to find some way to make Togepi happy!

Squirtle pointed to a nearby tree. A juicy apple hung from a high branch.

"*Pikachu!*" Pikachu said happily. Maybe Togepi was hungry. Togepi liked to eat apples.

But first they had to get the apple from the tree.

"*Bulbasaur!*" Two leaves whipped out of the bulb on Bulbasaur's back. Bulbasaur was using its Razor Leaf Attack to slice the apple from the branch.

"*Pika!*" Pikachu ran for the apple.

The apple rolled across the grass. It landed at Psyduck's feet. Psyduck picked up the apple.

"Psy?" Psyduck ate the apple in one gulp!

"Waaaaah!" Togepi cried and cried.

Pikachu did not know what to do. Ash was counting on it to take care of Togepi! And Pikachu could not even stop Togepi from crying.

This was supposed to be the best day ever. But it was starting out all wrong!

CHAPTER THREE

Pikachu Meets the Bullies

"Bulbasaur!" Bulbasaur walked up to Togepi. Two green vines shot from the bulb on its back. The vines picked up Togepi.

Bulbasaur swung Togepi gently in the air.

"Bulba, bulba," sang Bulbasaur softly. *"Hush, hush."*

Togepi stopped crying. Bulbasaur's lullaby was working!

Togepi fell asleep. Bulbasaur lowered Togepi onto a soft patch of grass.

Pikachu smiled at Squirtle and Bulbasaur. They did it!

Maybe this day would be a good day after all.

Just then, the peaceful silence was broken.

Pikachu spun around. A bunch of Pokémon were walking into the playground. They were talking and laughing loudly.

Pikachu knew these Pokémon.
They could be real bullies.

A Pokémon named Snubble led
the bullies. Snubble was a Fairy
Pokémon. It looked like a pink
bulldog. It seemed tough and
mean.

Raichu was the biggest bully of
the bunch. Raichu was a Lightning
Mouse Pokémon, just like Pikachu.
But Raichu was the evolved form
of Pikachu. It was bigger and had
powerful Shock Attacks.

Then there was Marril. This
blue Mouse Pokémon was small

and chubby. Unlike Pikachu and Raichu, it had Water powers.

Last was Cubone. This lonely Pokémon wore a skull mask on its face and carried a bone. Quiet and shy, Cubone was not friendly with many other Pokémon.

Pikachu faced the bullies.

"Pika! Pika!" Pikachu told them to be quiet so Togepi could sleep.

"Raichu!" Raichu just laughed. Raichu's friends joined in.

"Waaaaah!" The loud bullies woke up Togepi.

This made Squirtle angry.

"Squirtle! Squirtle!" Squirtle yelled at Raichu.

The bullies made angry faces. They faced Pikachu, Squirtle, and Bulbasaur.

"Raichu!"

"Snubble!"

"Marril!"

"Cubone!"

The bullies each gave a battle cry. They wanted to fight!

CHAPTER FOUR
Togepi Trouble!

Pikachu pushed itself between
the angry Pokémon.

"Pika! Pika!" Pikachu tried
to convince the Pokémon that
fighting was a bad idea. It would
set a bad example for baby Togepi.

Then a sound made Pikachu
stop.

"Togi! Togi!" It was Togepi. The little Pokémon was toddling down the road! It wanted to run and play.

"Pika!" Pikachu ran off after Togepi.

Togepi hopped down the trail. The path came to a deep canyon. At the bottom of the canyon was a rushing river.

A big log stretched from one side of the canyon to the other. Togepi hopped onto the log.

"Pika!" Pikachu ran as fast as it could. It had to catch Togepi before it fell off the log!

Pikachu and its friends are excited about their vacation!

Can Pikachu, Bulbasaur, Psyduck, and Squirtle cheer up Togepi?

Uh-oh,
Togepi
is crying!

Pikachu makes funny
faces for Togepi.

Togepi wants to play on the log . . .

. . . but then it starts to spin!

Uh-oh! Pikachu is headed for trouble!

It is a good thing Electric Pokémon can swim!

**Marril challenges Squirtle
to a race in the pool.**

And they are off!

Pikachu cheers Squirtle on!

Goldeen and Squirtle are going in the wrong direction!

Oh no! Marril wins the race.

Raichu vs. Pikachu — this battle is electric!

Uh-oh! The lightning Pokémon are stuck together.

**Meowth, Arbok, and Weezing
are on vacation, too.**

**Charizard
to the
rescue!**

Ouch! Charizard accidentally flies into a pipe — and gets its head stuck.

Teamwork! Pikachu and the bullies pull together to free Charizard.

Now that they are friends, all the Pokémon play together on the new slide and raft.

Pikachu and its new friends
say good-bye after a fun day
of adventure and play.

Pikachu hopped onto the log. It reached for Togepi. But the little Pokémon was too far ahead.

Then the log began to roll. It rolled along the canyon.

Pikachu tried to keep its balance. Up ahead, Togepi teetered back and forth.

Pikachu ran to Togepi. The log wobbled beneath them.

Pikachu ran too fast. Its feet slipped!

"Pikaaaaaaa!"

Pikachu screamed as it fell down to the river below.

CHAPTER FIVE
Who Is Tougher?

Splash! Pikachu landed in the river.

The river was moving fast. Pikachu swam with all its might. Puffing and panting, it crawled up to the shore.

But where was Togepi?

"Togi! Togi!"

Pikachu looked up. Togepi was all right! The tiny Pokémon had made it safely to the other side of the canyon.

Pikachu scrambled up the side of the canyon. It hugged Togepi.

"Pikachu!" Pikachu was happy that Togepi was safe.

Then, Pikachu remembered.

The bullies!

Pikachu picked up Togepi and ran back to its friends.

Squirtle and Snubble were face-to-face. They looked angry.

"*Squirtle! Squirtle! Squirtle!*"

Squirtle was challenging Snubble to a staring contest!

"*Snubble!*" The pink Pokémon agreed.

Snubble puffed up its chest. It tried to look tough.

Squirtle puffed up its chest, too. Then Squirtle puffed up its cheeks. Squirtle would show Snubble which of them was tougher!

But Squirtle puffed itself up so

much that it lost its balance.
Squirtle fell backward and crashed
to the ground.

"*Snubble!*" Snubble and its
friends laughed.

Bulbasaur stomped up and
faced Snubble.

"*Bulbasaur!*" Now Bulbasaur
wanted to challenge Snubble.

"*Snubble!*" Snubble gave
Bulbasaur its meanest stare.

Bulbasaur stared back. It rolled
its left eye. It rolled its right eye.
Bulbasaur's eyes spun around and
around.

Snubble got dizzy looking at Bulbasaur's eyes. The pink Pokémon swayed back and forth. Then Snubble fell to the ground!

Bulbasaur won!

Now Squirtle laughed at Snubble.

"Raichu!" Raichu faced Squirtle. Raichu looked very, very angry.

Marril pushed Raichu aside.

"Marril!" the blue Mouse Pokémon told Squirtle.

"Squirtle!" said Squirtle.

Pikachu groaned. Marril and

Squirtle both had Water powers. Now they were going to have a race in the Pokémon pool.

"Pika pi!" Pikachu pleaded. All Pikachu wanted was for everyone to be friends.

But Marril and Squirtle had made up their minds. They led the way to the Pokémon pool.

The pool was crowded with all kinds of Pokémon. Some Pokémon splashed and played. Others swam back and forth. And some just sat on the edge of the pool.

"Pika!" Pikachu waved to

Misty's Pokémon, Goldeen and Staryu. They were both swimming in the pool. Pikachu wanted them to know about the race.

Marril and Squirtle climbed onto two rocks at the end of the pool. They were ready to race.

Pikachu, Bulbasaur, and Togepi lined up at the other end to cheer for Squirtle. The bullies lined up next to them.

Pikachu began the countdown. *"Pi-ka-"*

"Boom!" Electrode, an Electric

Pokémon that looked like a ball, exploded behind them.

Marril and Squirtle dove into the water.

The race was on!

CHAPTER SIX
Pikachu Gets Angry

Marril and Squirtle swam through the water. Both Pokémon were fast!

First Squirtle took the lead.

Then Marril took the lead.

Then Squirtle passed Marril.

It was a close race!

Marril charged ahead. But there

was so much splashing water. Marril could not see where it was going.

Crash! Marril banged into Staryu by mistake.

The starfish-shaped Pokémon jumped out of the water. It was angry.

A blast of water shot out of the jewel in Staryu's middle. The water blast pushed Marril all the way back to the end of the pool.

Squirtle had a big lead now!

"Squirtle!" Squirtle laughed. Now it would win the race!

Squirtle swam toward the end of the pool. It moved fast.

But something was wrong.

Squirtle was moving backward!

Squirtle looked down. It was on top of Goldeen! It had swum onto Goldeen by mistake. Now Goldeen was swimming in the wrong direction.

"Squirtle!" Squirtle cried. Marril swam past Squirtle. The Mouse Pokémon now had the lead.

Squirtle jumped off Goldeen's back. It swam as fast as it could. But it was too late.

Marril touched the end of the pool first.

Marril won!

The bullies clapped and cheered for Marril.

Pikachu and Togepi hugged Squirtle.

"Pika pi!" Pikachu knew Squirtle did its best.

"Marril ril!" Marril laughed and pointed at Squirtle.

Squirtle stomped up to the bullies. Marril faced Squirtle. The two Water Pokémon glared at each other.

Now they *really* wanted to
fight!

"*Pikachu!*" Pikachu stepped
between them. Fighting would not
solve anything. They were
supposed to be having fun!

This was not the best day ever.
In fact, it was turning into the
worst day ever!

"*Rai rai rai!*" Raichu did not
like Pikachu butting in. Angry
sparks flew from Raichu's cheeks.
Raichu aimed the sparks at
Pikachu.

Raichu missed. The sparks hit baby Togepi by mistake!

"*Waaaah!*" Togepi cried.

Now Pikachu was angry.

Very angry.

No bully was going to hurt Togepi if Pikachu could help it.

"*Pikachuuuu!*" Now sparks flew from Pikachu's cheeks. Pikachu aimed the sparks at Raichu.

Raichu aimed *more* sparks at Pikachu.

The two Electric Pokémon got

closer and closer. Sparks flew between them.

Soon their cheeks were touching.

"Pikachu!"

"Raichu!"

Each Pokémon set off an electric charge.

Then a strange thing happened.

The electricity glued Pikachu's and Raichu's cheeks together.

The two Pokémon were stuck to one another!

CHAPTER SEVEN

Run, Pikachu, Run!

Meanwhile, high on the mountain, three Pokémon settled down for a nap.

Weezing, a Poison Pokémon, floated in the air. Weezing looked like a black cloud with two heads.

Arbok stretched its long body.

Arbok looked like a big, scary snake.

Meowth yawned. This talking Pokémon looked like a cat.

Meowth, Weezing, and Arbok all belonged to Team Rocket. Most of the time, they tried to help Team Rocket steal Pikachu from Ash. But not today. They were here to have fun and rest, like all the other Pokémon.

"Meowth! A day of rest at last," Meowth said. The Pokémon yawned again. "This is the perfect place for a catnap!"

Weezing and Arbok yawned, too. They curled up next to Meowth.

Soon they were all snoring away.

Back at the bottom of the mountain, Pikachu and Raichu were more angry than ever.

The two Pokémon pulled and pulled. It was no use.

They could not come unstuck!

Raichu and Pikachu ran as fast as they could. Maybe if they moved fast enough, they would come apart. The two Pokémon took off toward the trail that wound around the mountain. They flew up the trail.

They ran past Chansey. Usually this round pink Pokémon made other Pokémon happy. But Raichu and Pikachu did not even notice Chansey.

Raichu and Pikachu ran off the trail. They ran into a stream.

Bam! They knocked over Poliwag, a round Water Pokémon.

Bam! They knocked over Seel, a Pokémon that looked like a white seal.

Bam! They knocked over. Seaking, a Pokémon that looked like a big goldfish with a horn on its forehead.

Raichu and Pikachu ran faster and faster. They ran so fast that they climbed *up* a big waterfall in seconds!

The two Pokémon ran across the top of the mountain. A big maze made of bushes stretched out in front of them.

Raichu and Pikachu crashed through the maze.

Up ahead, Hitmonlee and

Hitmonchan played together. The Fighting Pokémon traded punches and kicks.

Crash! Raichu and Pikachu slammed right into them. Hitmonlee and Hitmonchan flew into the air.

Next, Raichu and Pikachu came to three Pokémon sleeping in the grass.

Meowth, Weezing, and Arbok!

Crash! Raichu and Pikachu slammed into the napping Pokémon.

Team Rocket's three Pokémon

went flying. They landed with a thud on the ground.

"I will get you, Pikachu!" Meowth yelled.

Raichu and Pikachu ran and ran. They ran back onto the trail. They wound their way back down the mountain.

Charizard was stretched out on the trail.

Raichu and Pikachu could not stop. They ran right over Charizard's tail.

The large Flying Pokémon jumped up. It roared. It pounded

its chest. Charizard ran after Raichu and Pikachu.

Raichu and Pikachu were fast, but Charizard was faster. Charizard ran past them. It blocked the trail.

Crash! Raichu and Pikachu slammed into Charizard.

The two Electric Pokémon flew backward. Finally, they came apart! They were not stuck together anymore!

Pikachu was happy — but not for long. Charizard was angry. It roared and flapped its wings.

Whoosh! The breeze sent
Raichu and Pikachu flying over the
edge of the trail.

They were falling to the bottom
of the mountain!

CHAPTER EIGHT

Look Out, Charizard!

Pikachu closed its eyes. It got ready to crash into the ground.

Boink!

Pikachu opened its eyes. Pikachu and Raichu had landed on Snorlax. This sleepy Pokémon had a big, round belly. Pikachu and Raichu bounced off its belly and landed gently on the ground.

Snorlax snored and rolled over on top of Raichu and Pikachu.

Pikachu and Raichu pushed their way out from under Snorlax. They stood up.

Pikachu's friends were there. Bulbasaur, Squirtle, and Togepi hugged Pikachu. Pidgeotto and Zubat flew around Pikachu. Vulpix licked Pikachu's face. Psyduck waddled around. Even Geodude and Onix smiled. They were all glad that Pikachu was safe.

The bullies were there, too. They walked up to Pikachu. Raichu still looked angry.

Pikachu glared at Raichu. This fight was not over!

"Char!"

Charizard's loud roar filled the air. The large Pokémon swept down from the top of the mountain. It ran right at Raichu and Pikachu!

Raichu and Pikachu jumped out of the way. Charizard looked back at them and laughed. It liked scaring the smaller Pokémon.

But Charizard was so busy scaring Pikachu and Raichu, it did not see where it was going. Just ahead was a lookout tower made of logs and ropes. Past the tower, a bunch of old pipes were sticking out of the mountain.

"Pika pi!" Pikachu tried to warn Charizard.

It was too late. Charizard crashed into the lookout tower. Logs tumbled everywhere.

Then Charizard flew right into

one of the pipes. Its head got
stuck!

Charizard pulled and pulled.
But it could not get out.

Charizard's head was trapped
inside the pipe!

CHAPTER NINE
Save Charizard!

Charizard roared loudly. It flapped its wings. It thumped its tail on the ground.

It was no use. Charizard could not get its head out of the pipe.

Pikachu turned to its friends.

"Pikachu! Pika pika pi!" Pikachu told them. Charizard had

been trying to scare them. But Pikachu and its friends knew they still had to help free Charizard!

Squirtle ran and found a rope. Pikachu tied the rope to one of Charizard's back legs.

Pikachu tied one end of the rope around Pidgeotto and Zubat. The two flying Pokémon flapped their wings and pulled as hard as they could.

Onix chomped on the other end of the rope. The giant Rock Pokémon pulled with all its might.

Pikachu, Squirtle, Bulbasaur,

Vulpix, and Geodude grabbed onto the rope. They all pulled as hard as they could.

Even baby Togepi helped!

Pikachu and its friends pulled and pulled.

Charizard roared. Fire flew out of its mouth and blew out the end of one of the pipes.

Its head was still stuck.

The Pokémon pulled harder. Charizard jerked forward. Pikachu and the other Pokémon flew back and landed on the ground with a thump.

"Rai rai rai!" Raichu and the other bullies laughed and laughed.

Pikachu turned to the bullies. Charizard needed help badly. Pikachu and its friends could not do it alone. They needed the bullies to help them.

"Pikachu," Pikachu pleaded. *"Pika pi. Pika pika pi."* Pikachu tried to make the bullies understand. If they all worked together, they could save Charizard.

The bullies stopped laughing. They looked at one another.

Finally, Raichu spoke up.

"*Rai rai rai rai!*" Raichu said. It smiled.

"*Marril!*" agreed Marril.

Snubble nodded. "*Snubble!*"

The three bullies stepped up and grabbed onto the rope. Only Cubone stayed aside. The quiet Pokémon was too shy to join in.

The other Pokémon took their places on the rope again. They pulled and pulled.

With the bullies' help, they were stronger. But they *still* could not free Charizard.

"*Char, char.*" Inside the pipe,

Charizard began to cry. Its sad sobs filled the playground.

Pikachu felt like crying, too. It had promised Ash that it would take care of all of its friends. And now Charizard was going to be trapped forever!

CHAPTER 10
Pokémon Power

From the sidelines, Cubone listened to Charizard cry. It did not like to see anybody sad.

Cubone did not feel so shy anymore. The Pokémon took a deep breath. It grabbed onto the rope.

"Pika!"

At Pikachu's cry, all of the Pokémon gave one mighty pull.

It worked! Charizard's head popped out of the pipe.

Charizard flew backward. All of the Pokémon went flying up, up into the air. They landed with a splash in the pool.

Above them, Meowth woke up from its nap again.

"That is it!" Meowth yelled. "I came here for some peace and quiet. The rest of you are making too much noise. I am going to come down there and fight you all!

You will never forget the day
you —"

Meowth could not finish.
Charizard came falling back down
to earth. *Slam!* The Flying
Pokémon landed on Meowth with
a crash.

Charizard got up and flew away.
Meowth wobbled to its feet.

"That is all right," Meowth said.
"I think I have had enough rest
today!"

Back down in the pool, the
Pokémon laughed and cheered.

"Pikachu!" Pikachu said

happily. It reached out a hand to Raichu. *"Pika pi?"*

"Rai!" Raichu shook Pikachu's hand. They were friends. There would be no more fighting.

Then Pikachu got an idea.

"Pika pika pi!" Pikachu told the others. Pikachu pointed to the pile of broken logs and ropes. If they could save Charizard, imagine the other things they could do together!

The other Pokémon liked Pikachu's idea. They grabbed the

logs. They grabbed the rope. They worked and worked. Before long, they were done.

The Pokémon had built fun new rides for the Pokémon Playground!

Pikachu and Squirtle swung on the new swing set.

Togepi and Vulpix played in the new sandbox.

Bulbasaur and Geodude slid down the new slide.

Charizard wanted to go on the new seesaw. The bullies helped out. Raichu, Marril, Snubble,

and Cubone got on one end of
the seesaw. But they still
were not heavy enough to lift
Charizard!

When the Pokémon got tired of
playing, they all jumped in the
pool. They played and splashed
together.

Soon the sun started to set. Red
streaked across the blue sky.
Pikachu could not believe the day
was almost over.

Suddenly, Ash's voice carried
into the playground.

"Pikachu, it is time to leave!" Ash yelled.

"Goldeen! Staryu! Psyduck! Come on back!" Misty called out.

"Geodude! Onix! Zubat! Vulpix! We have to go!" Brock cried.

Pikachu and the others jumped out of the pool. Pikachu turned and looked at the bullies. They were not bullies anymore. They were friends. Pikachu would miss them.

"Pika pi!" Pikachu waved good-bye to Raichu, Marril,

Snubble, and Cubone. The Pokémon waved back.

Then Pikachu ran down the trail. Pikachu might miss its new friends, but there was someone Pikachu missed even more.

"Pikachu!" Ash cried.

Pikachu jumped into Ash's arms. The yellow Pokémon gave Ash a big hug.

"Did you take good care of the other Pokémon?" Ash asked.

Pikachu nodded. Pikachu's friends nodded, too.

"I knew I could count on you, Pikachu!" Ash hugged Pikachu.

Pikachu smiled.

This really *was* the best day ever!

About the Author

Tracey West has been writing books for more than ten years. When she is not playing the blue version of the Pokémon game (she started with a Squirtle), she enjoys reading comic books, watching cartoons, and taking long walks in the woods (looking for wild Pokémon). She lives in a small town in New York with her family and pets.